MR. CLEVER

by Roger Hargreaves

KT-555-731

WORLD INTERNATIONAL

Mr Clever was quite the cleverest person ever.

The Cleverest Person In The World!

And, he knew it!

"Oh, I am so very very CLEVER," he used to say.

To himself more often than not.

He lived in Cleverland where, as you may know, everybody and everything is as clever as can be.

In Cleverland clever trees manage to grow apples and oranges at the same time!

In Cleverland clever flowers get up and go for a walk!

Clever worms drive around in cars all day!

And clever elephants play tennis!

Oh yes, Cleverland is quite the most clever place.

Would you like to live there?

Mr Clever does.

"Oh, I am so very very CLEVER to build such a clever house," he used to go around telling everybody.

One morning, Mr Clever was awakened by his special Mr Clever alarm clock.

Not only did it wake you up by ringing a bell: it also switched on a light; and said "Good morning"; and made a cup of tea; and showed what the weather was going to be; and told you the time; and showed you the date. It also whistled cheerfully while it was doing all that!

Mr Clever yawned, got up, washed, cleaned his teeth (with his special Mr Clever toothbrush which squeezed toothpaste on to the brush out of the handle), and went downstairs for breakfast.

He popped a slice of bread into his special Mr Clever electric toaster.

Which not only toasted the bread, but also spread it with butter and marmalade, AND cut off the crusts!

After breakfast he went for a long walk.

An extremely long walk.

In fact, such a long walk that he walked all the way out of Cleverland, although he didn't know it.

He met somebody who was also out for a walk.

Do you know who it was?

That's right.

Mr Happy!

"Hello," cried Mr Clever. "I'm The Cleverest Person In The World!"

"Oh good," said Mr Happy. "Then you must be clever enough to make up a really good joke to tell me."

He laughed.

"Jokes make me happy," he explained.

Mr Clever's face fell.

"I don't know any jokes," he admitted.

"Well, that's not very clever of you, is it?" said Mr Happy, and went off.

Mr Clever went on.

And do you know who he met next?

That's right.

Mr Greedy!

"Hello," cried Mr Clever. "I'm The Cleverest Person In The World!"

"Oh good," said Mr Greedy. "Then you can tell me the recipe of the world's most delicious dish."

He licked his lips.

"I like food," he explained.

Mr Clever's face fell.

"I can't cook," he admitted. "And I don't know any recipes!"

"Well, that's not very clever of you, is it?" said Mr Greedy, and went off.

In search of food.

Mr Clever went on.

And who do you think he met next?

Yes.

Mr Forgetful!

"Hello," cried Mr Clever. "I'm The Cleverest Person In The World!"

"Oh good," said Mr Forgetful. "Then you can tell me what my name is."

He smiled apologetically.

"I've forgotten," he explained.

Mr Clever's face fell for the third time that morning.

"But I don't know your name," he admitted. "We've only just met!"

"Well, that's not very clever of you, is it?" said Mr Forgetful, and he too went off.

Forgetting to say goodbye!

And so it went on. All day.

Mr Clever couldn't tell Mr Sneeze the cure for a cold.

And he couldn't tell Mr Small how he could grow bigger.

And he couldn't tell Mr Jelly what the secret of being brave was.

And he couldn't tell Mr Topsy-Turvy how to talk the round way right.

I mean the right way round.

A not very clever day!

Not at all.

Not a bit.

As by now he wasn't feeling anything like The Cleverest Person In The World, Mr Clever decided he'd better go home.

He passed a pair of worms who were having a chat.

"Who's that?" asked one worm.

"That," replied the other worm, "is Mr Clever, The Cleverest Person In The World, on his way home to Cleverland!"

The first worm thought.

"He can't be that clever," he replied . . .

. . . "he's going the wrong way!"

MORE SPECIAL OFFERS
FOR MR MEN AND LITTLE MISS READERS

In every Mr Men and Little Miss book like this one, <u>and now</u> in the Mr Men sticker and activity books, you will find a special token. Collect six tokens and we will send you a gift of your choice.

Choose either a <u>Mr Men</u> or <u>Little Miss</u> poster, <u>or</u> a Mr Men or Little Miss **double sided** *full colour bedroom door hanger.*

Return this page <u>with six tokens per gift required</u> to
Marketing Dept., MM / LM Gifts, World International Ltd., Deanway Technology Centre, Wilmslow Road, Handforth, Cheshire SK9 3FB

|—— 100 mm ——|

Your name:_____ Age: _____

Address: _____

_____

_____Postcode: _____

Parent / Guardian Name (Please Print) _____

Please tape a 20p coin to your request to cover part post and package cost

I enclose <u>six</u> tokens per gift, please send me:-

ENTRANCE FEE
3 SAUSAGES

250 mm

MR. GREEDY

Posters:-	Mr Men Poster	☐	Little Miss Poster	☐
Door Hangers -	Mr Nosey / Muddle	☐	Mr Greedy / Lazy	☐
	Mr Tickle / Grumpy	☐	Mr Slow / Busy	☐
	Mr Messy / Quiet	☐		
	L Miss Fun / Late	☐	L Miss Helpful / Tidy	☐
	L Miss Busy / Brainy	☐	L Miss Star / Fun	☐

Please Tick Appropriate Box

Collect six of these tokens
You will find one inside every
Mr Men and Little Miss book
which has this special offer.

1
TOKEN

We may occasionally wish to advise you of other Mr Men gifts.
If you would rather we didn't please tick this box ☐

Mr Men and Little Miss Library Presentation Boxes

In response to the many thousands of requests for the above, we are delighted to advise that these are now available direct from ourselves, for only £4.99 (inc VAT) plus 50p p & p. The full colour units accommodate each complete library. They have an integral carrying handle and "push out" bookmark as well as a neat stay closed fastener.

Please do not send cash in the post. Cheques should be made payable to **World International Ltd.** **for the sum of £5.49** (inc p & p) per box.

Return this page with your cheque, stating below which presentation box you would like, **to Mr Men Office, World International Ltd.,** **Deanway Technology Centre, Wilmslow Road, Handforth, Cheshire SK9 3FB.**

Your Name _____

Your Address _____

_____

_____Post Code _____

Name of Parent/Guardian (please print) _____

Signature _____

I enclose a cheque for £ _____ made payable to World International Ltd.

Please send me a Mr Men Presentation Box ⬜ (please tick or write in quantity)

Little Miss Presentation Box ⬜

Thank you

Offer applies to UK, Eire & Channel Isles only.